DISNEY·PIXAR
MONSTERS, INC.

Adapted by Chuck Wilson
Illustrated by the Disney Storybook Artists

 A GOLDEN BOOK • NEW YORK

Late one night, a little boy awoke to see . . . a monster!
The boy SCREAMED!

Then the monster **SCREAMED,** too!

With a sigh, the Scare teacher turned off the mechanical boy and the simulator machine. Then she reminded the students of Monsters, Inc., of the rules: Never scream. And never leave a child's closet door open—a child could get into Monstropolis! The students knew that the screams they collected from human kids powered their city. But they also knew that children and their belongings were toxic!

Meanwhile, across town, James P. Sullivan was exercising. His assistant and best friend, Mike Wazowski, stood nearby, coaching him.

Sulley, as Sullivan was called, was a professional Scarer at Monsters, Inc. He needed to stay in top shape for the physical demands of his job.

"Feel the burn," Mike urged. "You call yourself a **MONSTER**?"

Sulley was **FAMOUS** for collecting more screams than any
other monster. His scaring skills were especially important
now—the city was in the middle of an energy shortage. Human
kids were getting harder to scare, and Monstropolis needed all
the screams it could get.

In the locker room at Monsters, Inc., Mike and Sulley prepared for their workday. A chameleonlike monster named Randall suddenly appeared.

"**AHHHH!**" Mike shrieked.

Randall was creepy and mean . . . and was very jealous of Sulley. Randall would do anything to be the company's top Scarer.

As the monsters made their way to the Scare Floor, they passed Roz, who was in charge of all the paperwork. Mike was **ALWAYS** late with his paperwork.

"I'm watching you, Wazowski," Roz growled at Mike. "Always watching."

On the Scare Floor, a giant conveyor belt dropped a child's closet door into each scare station. A Scarer entered a child's bedroom through the door, then did his best to scare the child and collect the screams.

Sulley walked in on a slumber party! He scared all the kids and filled many canisters with screams. As Sulley's scream total shot to the top of the Scare Leader Board, Randall snarled. He hated coming in second.

Suddenly, an **EMERGENCY** bell rang. A Scarer named George had returned from the human world with a child's sock on his back!

In seconds, a squad from the Child Detection Agency, also known as the CDA, arrived to decontaminate him. Poor George!

While the Scare Floor was shut down for cleanup, Sulley talked to Mr. Waternoose, the head of Monsters, Inc. Mr. Waternoose was worried that the company couldn't supply enough power for the city.

To help out, Sulley promised to demonstrate proper scaring techniques to the new Scare recruits.

After work, Mike rushed to meet his girlfriend,
Celia, for dinner. But Roz blocked his way.

"I'm sure you filed your paperwork, right?"
rasped the cranky clerk.

Mike had forgotten! Now he was going to be
late for his date with Celia. Luckily, Sulley offered
to file the paperwork for him.

When Sulley went back to the Scare Floor to get the papers, he noticed that someone had left a door out. He peeked inside but didn't see any monsters.

Then something grabbed his tail. It was . . . a **CHILD!**

Sulley tried to toss the little girl back into her bedroom, but she wanted to play. She giggled and chased Sulley around, calling, "KITTY!"

Sulley finally managed to put the child into a duffel bag. He raced back to the Scare Floor and saw Randall. The sneaky monster pushed a button and sent the girl's door back to storage. What was Sulley going to do?

Sulley went to the restaurant where Mike and Celia were having dinner. As he tried to explain what was going on, the child got out of the bag.

"**BOO!**" she shouted, giggling.

All the monsters screamed. When the CDA arrived, Mike and Sulley scooped the girl up in a take-out container and ran.

At their apartment, Sulley and Mike tried to keep their distance from the girl. They were **TERRIFIED** of her! Then Mike tripped, and the little girl laughed. As she giggled, the lights in the room burned brighter and brighter—until they burned out with a **POP**! If that happened again, the CDA would surely find them.

After a long night, Sulley put the child to bed. But she was afraid that something was in the closet. She drew a picture of what scared her. It was Randall!

Sulley stayed with her until she fell asleep. Then he went to talk to Mike.

"This might sound crazy," he said, "but I don't think the kid's dangerous. What if we just put her back in her door?"

The next morning, Sulley disguised the girl as a little monster. Then he, Mike, and the girl all walked straight into Monsters, Inc.

Sulley told everyone that she was a relative. They believed him!

As Mike tried to figure out how to find the girl's door, Randall showed up. Sulley and Mike heard him order his assistant to "get the machine up and running." Then he said he would "take care of the girl."

Sulley knew that the girl, whom he had started to call Boo, needed to go home quickly!

In the hallway, Mike was cornered by Randall.
"Where's the KID?" he demanded.

Mike said he didn't know, but Randall didn't believe him. Randall told Mike that he would have the kid's door waiting on the Scare Floor so she could get back to the human world.

Sulley was worried when he heard the plan. To prove it was safe, Mike went through Boo's door first—and was captured by Randall!

Sulley and Boo quietly followed Randall to a hidden laboratory. Randall had invented a scary-looking machine that could pull screams out of kids . . . and he was about to test it on Mike!

Sulley rescued Mike just in time. The friends raced to warn Mr. Waternoose about Randall's evil plans.

Waternoose was **SHOCKED** to see Boo. "It's not our fault—it's Randall's!" Mike cried.

But Waternoose already knew about Randall's plan . . . because he was in on it! He grabbed Boo and shoved Sulley and Mike through an open door and into the human world. They were banished from Monstropolis!

Mike and Sulley ended up in the Himalayas, where they met another banished MONSTER—the Abominable Snowman.

But Sulley didn't want to chat. Boo needed help! He made a sled and raced toward the local village. There he found a closet door that led him back to Monsters, Inc.

Sulley **BURST** onto the Scare Floor. He ran to the secret lab, where he smashed Randall's horrible scream extractor machine to pieces. As Sulley escaped with Boo, Mike caught up with them.

Sulley, Mike, and Boo were on the run from Randall. To slow Randall down, Celia announced over the loudspeaker that Randall was the new Top Scarer. The mean monster was instantly mobbed by cheering coworkers.

Randall could only watch with a frown as Sulley, Mike, and Boo jumped onto the door conveyor belt.

Suddenly, the power went **OUT**, and the conveyor belt stopped moving! Randall was able to make his way closer to Mike, Sulley, and Boo by jumping from door to door.

"Make her laugh!" Sulley shouted. Mike quickly made some silly faces. When Boo giggled, the power returned.

Randall still managed to catch up with them.
He grabbed Boo—but she fought back!
"She's not **SCARED** of you anymore," Sulley said.
Finally, Mike and Sulley kicked Randall through a
door and then smashed it. He was gone for good.
Next, Sulley and Mike tricked Mr. Waternoose
into talking about his evil plan as Mike recorded
him. "I'll kidnap a thousand children before I let
this company die!" Waternoose shouted.

Soon **EVERYONE** in Monstropolis had heard about
Waternoose's wicked plan. He was arrested by the
head of the CDA—who turned out to be Roz!

It was time for Boo to go home. The little girl gave Mike a hug before following Sulley into her room. He gently tucked her into bed.

Sadly, Sulley said goodbye and returned to Monsters, Inc. Roz ordered the CDA to shred Boo's door. It couldn't be used for scaring anymore, which meant Sulley would never be able to visit Boo again.

Sulley became the new president of Monsters, Inc. And the Scare Floor became a Laugh Floor instead. Sulley solved the energy shortage by proving that kids' laughter produced more power than their screams. And Mike became the company's top Laugh Collector.

One day, Mike had a big surprise for Sulley. He had put Boo's door back together! Sulley opened the door and Boo called out, "KITTY!" The friends were reunited at last.